THE POP DUET

Level 3E

Written by Deborah Chancellor
Illustrated by Alex Paterson
Reading Consultant: Betty Franchi

About Phonics

Spoken English uses more than 40 speech sounds.
Each sound is called a *phoneme*. Some phonemes relate
to a single letter (d-o-g) and others to combinations
of letters (sh-ar-p). When a phoneme is written down,
it is called a *grapheme*. Teaching these sounds, matching
them to their written form, and sounding out words for
reading is the basis of phonics.

Early phonics instruction gives children the tools to sound
out, blend, and say the words without having to rely on
memory or guesswork. This instruction gives children the
confidence and ability to read unfamiliar words, helping
them progress toward independent reading.

About the Consultant

Betty Franchi is an American educator with
a Bachelor's Degree in Elementary and Middle
Education as well as a Master's Degree in Special
Education. Betty holds a National Boards for
Professional Teaching Standards certification.
Throughout her 24 years as a teacher, she has
studied and developed an expertise in Phonetic
Awareness and has implemented phonetic strategies,
teaching many young children to read, including
students with special needs.

Reading tips

This book focuses on the *ue* sound as in cue.

Tricky and/or new words in this book

Any words in bold may have unusual spellings or are new and have not yet been introduced.

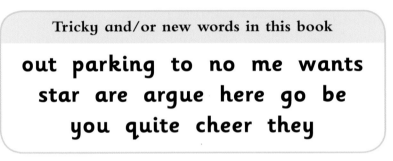

Tricky and/or new words in this book

out parking to no me wants star are argue here go be you quite cheer they

Extra ways to have fun with this book

After the readers have finished the story, ask them questions about what they have just read.

How did Jess and Zack travel to perform the duet?
Why was Jess sad in the middle of the story?

Explain that the two letters *ue* make one sound. Think of other words that make the *ue* sound, such as *venue* and *duet*.

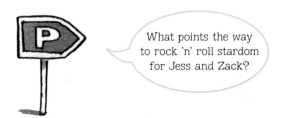

What points the way to rock 'n' roll stardom for Jess and Zack?

A Pronunciation Guide

This grid highlights the sounds used in the story and offers a guide on how to say them.

s	a	t	p	i
as in sat	as in ant	as in tin	as in pig	as in ink
n	c	e	h	r
as in net	as in cat	as in egg	as in hen	as in rat
m	d	g	o	u
as in mug	as in dog	as in get	as in ox	as in up
l	f	b	j	v
as in log	as in fan	as in bag	as in jug	as in van
w	z	y	k	qu
as in wet	as in zip	as in yet	as in kit	as in quick
x	ff	ll	ss	zz
as in box	as in off	as in ball	as in kiss	as in buzz
ck	pp	nn	rr	gg
as in duck	as in puppy	as in bunny	as in arrow	as in egg
dd	bb	tt	sh	ch
as in daddy	as in chubby	as in attic	as in shop	as in chip
th	th	ng	nk	le
as in them	as in the	as in sing	as in sunk	as in bottle
ai	ee	ie	oa	ue
as in rain	as in feet	as in pies	as in oak	as in cue

Be careful not to add an /uh/ sound to /s/, /t/, /p/, /c/, /h/, /r/, /m/, /d/, /g/, /l/, /f/ and /b/. For example, say /ff/ not /fuh/ and /sss/ not /suh/.

Jess **wants to be** a pop **star**.

"Can **you** sing a duet with **me**?" she asks Zack.

Zack groans. "Buzz off!" he says.
"Duets **are no** fun."

Jess and Zack **argue**,
but Jess gets her way.

Zack agrees to sing
a duet at a pop gig.

The pop gig is at a big venue.

Jess and Zack **go** by
bus to the venue.

14

The bus runs **out** of gas on the way. It stops in a **parking** lot.

Jess and Zack are stuck.
They cannot get to the venue.

Jess is **quite** sad. She still
wants to sing her duet.

Zack tries to cheer up Jess.
"Let's sing the duet **here**," he says.

The duet is a hit. The kids on the bus **cheer**.

"This duet is cool!" they say.

Jess and Zack sing the duet again.
"We don't need a big venue,"
Jess cries.

"I think duets are fun after all,"
Zack says.

OVER **48** TITLES IN SIX LEVELS
Betty Franchi recommends...

Some titles from Level 1

I love reading phonics **Bad Rat**
978 1 84898 747 0

I love reading phonics **The Best Gift**
978 1 84898 750 0

I love reading phonics **Clint and Grant Play I-Spy**
978 1 84898 752 4

I love reading phonics **Bret and Grandma's Trip!**
978 1 84898 751 7

Some titles from Level 2

I love reading phonics **Wish Fish**
978 1 84898 755 5

I love reading phonics **Chuck and Duck**
978 1 84898 756 2

I love reading phonics **Pink Bunny**
978 1 84898 760 9

I love reading phonics **Let's go to the Swings**
978 1 84898 759 3

Other titles to enjoy from Level 3

I love reading phonics **Bart's Go-Cart**
978 1 84898 768 5

I love reading phonics **Queen Ella's Feet**
978 1 84898 764 7

I love reading phonics **Puff Flies**
978 1 84898 765 4

An Hachette Company
First Published in the United States by TickTock, an imprint of Octopus Publishing Group.
www.octopusbooksusa.com

Copyright © Octopus Publishing Group Ltd 2013

Distributed in the US by
Hachette Book Group USA
237 Park Avenue, New York NY 10017, USA

Distributed in Canada by
Canadian Manda Group
165 Dufferin Street, Toronto, Ontario, Canada M6K 3H6

ISBN 978 1 84898 767 8

Printed and bound in China
10 9 8 7 6 5 4 3 2 1

4 1 4 8 2

4148218